Green Light Readers
For the new reader who's ready to GO!

Amazing adventures await every young child who is eager to read.

Green Light Readers encourage children to explore, to imagine, and to grow through books. Created for beginning readers at two levels of skill, these lively illustrated stories have been carefully developed to reinforce reading basics taught at school and to make reading a fun and rewarding experience for children and grown-ups to share outside the classroom.

The grades and ages within each skill level are general guidelines only, and books included in both levels may feature any or all of the bulleted characteristics. When choosing a book for a new reader, remember that every child progresses at his or her own pace—be patient and supportive as the magic of reading takes hold.

❶ Buckle up!
Kindergarten–Grade 1: Developing reading skills, ages 5–7
- Short, simple stories • Fully illustrated • Familiar objects and situations
- Playful rhythms • Spoken language patterns of children
- Rhymes and repeated phrases • Strong link between text and art

2 Start the engine!
Grades 1–2: Reading with help, ages 6–8
- Longer stories, including nonfiction • Short chapters
- Generously illustrated • Less-familiar situations
- More fully developed characters • Creative language, including dialogue
- More subtle link between text and art

Green Light Readers incorporate characteristics detailed in the Reading Recovery model used by educators to assess the readability of texts through the end of first grade. Guidelines for reading levels for these readers have been developed with assistance from Mary Lou Meerson. An educational consultant, Ms. Meerson has been a classroom teacher, a language arts coordinator, an elementary school principal, and a university professor.

Published in collaboration with Harcourt School Publishers

Big Pig
and
Little Pig

Big Pig
and Little Pig

David McPhail

Green Light Readers
Harcourt, Inc.
San Diego   New York   London

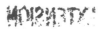

www.harcourt.com

First Green Light Readers edition 2001
Green Light Readers is a trademark of Harcourt, Inc., registered in the United States of America and/or other jurisdictions.

Library of Congress Cataloging-in-Publication Data
McPhail, David M.
Big Pig and Little Pig/by David McPhail.
p. cm.
"Green Light Readers."
Summary: Although they like different things,
Big Pig and Little Pig enjoy spending time together.
[1. Pigs—Fiction. 2. Friendship—Fiction.] I. Title. II. Green Light reader.
PZ7.M2427Bi 2001
[E]—dc21 00-9725
ISBN 0-15-216516-9
ISBN 0-15-216510-X (pb)

C E G H F D
A C E G H F D B (pb)

EXTENSION

"I am hot," said Big Pig.

"Me, too," said Little Pig.

"I am going to make a pool,"
said Big Pig.

"Me, too," said Little Pig.

"I am going to dig a hole,"
said Big Pig.

"Me, too," said Little Pig.

"I am going to get a bucket,"
said Big Pig.

"Me, too," said Little Pig.

"I am going to fill up the pool,"
said Big Pig.

"Me, too," said Little Pig.

"Now I can sit back down," said Big Pig.

"Me, too!" said Little Pig.

Meet the Author-Illustrator

David McPhail loves to draw pigs. When he was a child, his favorite character was the pig in the book **Charlotte's Web**. *"Pigs tickle me," he says. "They're fun because they do such silly things!" He hopes you giggled when you read* **Big Pig and Little Pig***!*

© Rick Friedman

David McPhail